My Pancakes Taste Different Today!

Heather Wood Galpert and Bruce Galpert

ILLUSTRATED BY Barbara Cate

Wagon Wheel Productions • Santa Fe, New Mexico

Ethan loves pancakes. His favorite breakfast
before going fishing at the nearby lake—a tall stack
of steaming hot pancakes—was waiting for him
on the kitchen table.

He loves pouring syrup slowly over his pancakes,
and watching it make little lakes and rivers
on his plate.

"Mom, these are the very best pancakes in the Whole Wide World," Ethan exclaimed before taking another big bite.

"And you can **THANK** the Whole Wide World for helping me make them," his mom smiled back.

"Thank the clouds for bringing the rain that fills our lake.
Thank the fish and snails that live in our lake and keep
the water clear and clean. Thank Mr. and Mrs. Beaver,
whose dams form the ponds in the river that water the
fields of wheat. Thank Farmer Tom who plants the
seeds and harvests the fields of wheat."

"You can thank the sun that helps Farmer Tom's wheat grow tall and golden, and remember to thank the mill that grinds the wheat into the pancake flour that we bring home from the grocery store."

Ethan was ready to go out and thank
Nature and Farmer Tom . . . and to catch the
biggest fish at the lake!
He headed towards his favorite fishing spot.

"Thank you, Farmer Tom, for planting
seeds and growing the fields of wheat.

Thank you, Mr. and Mrs. Beaver.
Your dams make the ponds in our river
that water the wheat fields.

Thank you, sun, because of you
the wheat grows tall and golden."

Ethan waved and shouted,
"Thank you, mill, for making the wheat
into my pancake flour!"

Ethan felt even happier after thanking everyone.

At the edge of the lake, he picked up a
stick and playfully tossed it into the tall grass.
He laughed as brightly colored birds
darted off in every direction.
The world looked magical today.

When he found his favorite fishing spot,
Ethan picked up a flat, shiny stone and skipped
it across the water. The fish jumped, which made
Ethan laugh some more. Many fish swirled around
the surface to catch the bread crumbs that he
sprinkled in the water.

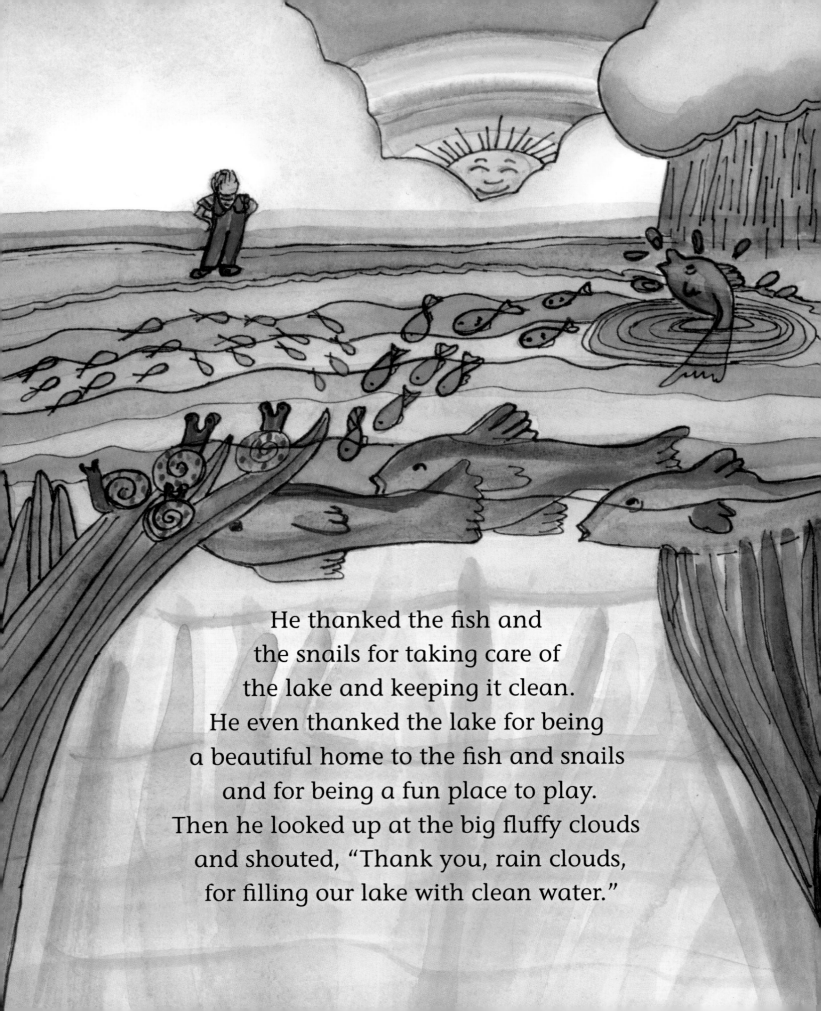

He thanked the fish and
the snails for taking care of
the lake and keeping it clean.
He even thanked the lake for being
a beautiful home to the fish and snails
and for being a fun place to play.
Then he looked up at the big fluffy clouds
and shouted, "Thank you, rain clouds,
for filling our lake with clean water."

Farmer Tom's tractor was parked at the edge of the
field near the lake. Ethan spotted an oil can on the
ground next to the tractor. Surely another big splash
in the lake would be a fun ending to the day.
He picked up the oily can, and as hard as he could,
threw it into the middle of the lake.

SPLASH!

It was the biggest splash he had ever made.
Ethan trotted home with a wide grin.

What Ethan did not know was that throwing that
oily can into the lake was about to change his
Whole Wide World—and his pancakes!

That oily can in the middle of the lake
began to leak gooey, dark **OOZE** into the water.
The **OOZE** slowly crept across the water and covered
many unhappy fish. Some were unable to swim.
The **OOZE** didn't stop there. It flowed into the river
where Mr. and Mrs. Beaver lived.

The beavers were scared of the **OOZE** seeping into the river; they ran to hide in the woods.

The ugly **OOZE** kept inching and flowing in every direction across the lake and into the fields of wheat, seeping into the soil. The wheat was no longer so golden. Those brightly colored birds were no longer bright and colorful.

The mill continued turning the wheat
into pancake flour not knowing that the
OOZE was deep in the roots of the wheat.
They delivered the flour to the grocery
store where Ethan and his mother
always buy their groceries.

Days passed and Ethan was ready for another
fishing trip to the lake. His prized pancake breakfast was
waiting for him in the kitchen. Ethan took his first big bite.
"YUK! My pancakes taste different today!"
he shouted, making an awful face.

Ethan was sad and confused. He sat at the kitchen
table and thought hard about why his pancakes
tasted different today. "I don't understand.
I thanked the clouds, the beavers, the fish and snails.
I thanked the sun and Farmer Tom and the mill.
I even thanked the lake! What happened?"

He thought about this, pouring the syrup slowly over his pancakes, watching it form lakes and rivers on his plate. This made him think about his own lake. And then he remembered that oil can and the

BIG SPLASH!

Ethan opened the kitchen
window and shouted out to all
the children in the neighborhood,
"I know why my pancakes
taste different today!
Hurry everyone,
hurry, come with me!"

Ethan and his friends hurried past
Farmer Tom who was looking so sad standing in
his wheat field smothered with

OOZE.

"We will fix this mess! Farmer Tom, don't you worry."
They hurried along the river, past the beaver dams,
all the way to the lake, and there they saw it!
The **OOZE** by now was wide and ugly
and it covered the entire lake.

"Let's get that OOZE!"

Ethan cried out, and all the children began to clean up the lake. They scrubbed each and every rock, carefully cleaned every fish, and shoveled up dirty sand until there was not even a speck of OOZE left.

Finally the **OOZE** was all gone!
Everyone stood back and admired the clean water in
the lake, watching it flow into the river and the fields.
They were excited when they saw Mr. and Mrs. Beaver
happily back in the river at work building another dam.

"Thank you children," Farmer Tom called out as they passed him standing in his field where he had already planted a new crop of healthy wheat.

Ethan cried out, "Let's have a party to celebrate, a Pancake Party!" Ethan gathered his friends together to thank them for helping to clean up the lake.

At the lakeside, Ethan's mom
served steaming, hot stacks of
fresh, fluffy pancakes to everyone.

This time, Ethan took a first big bite of his
pancakes, smiled and said, "YUMMMMMM!"
"These are the best pancakes in the
Whole . . . Wide . . . World. Thank YOU, Mom!"

Outside, under a bright blue sky, Ethan and his friends enjoyed a pancake feast to celebrate a clean and happy Earth.

Fluffy Pancakes

(without **OOZE!**)

Organic, local and sustainable ingredients are recommended—we think they taste better, too!

1 ¼ cups flour (if gluten free we suggest King Arthur Flour Gluten Free Multi-Purpose Flour)
¼ cup sugar
1 ¼ teaspoon baking powder
1 teaspoon baking soda
1 large egg
1 ⅓ cup buttermilk
¼ cup melted butter

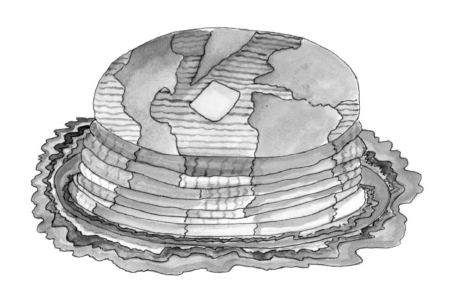

Ask an adult to help you make Fluffy Pancakes! Measure all the ingredients out separately. Whisk the dry ingredients together until combined. In a small bowl, whisk the egg into the milk. Add the milk and egg combination to the dry ingredients then add the melted (but not hot) butter. Don't over mix; a few lumps in batter is fine. Lightly grease a large skillet over medium heat (vegetable oil spray is easy to use) and add ¼ cup of the batter to form each pancake. Cook until the first side is golden brown, or until the top surface bubbles and is dotted with holes. Flip and cook until the other side is golden brown. Serve hot with lots of maple syrup and share with your friends and family. Yum! Have fun cleaning up the kitchen after you enjoy your pancakes.

Compliments of Chef Johnny Vee • www.ChefJohnnyVee.com

This book is dedicated to the Earth
and all that care for it.

First Edition 2016
ISBN 978-0-9974841-0-6

Printed in the USA

This book was typeset in ITC Stone Informal.
The illustrations were done in watercolor.

Wagon Wheel Productions
Santa Fe, New Mexico

Visit our website at www.ThePancakesBook.com
email: info@ThePancakesBook.com
www.WagonWheelProductions.com

Illustrations by Barbara Cate:
www.mesamooncards.com

Book design by Ann Lowe